STRICHEN SCHOOL

The Shadow on the Stairs

by

Ann Halam

Illustrated by Edmund Bright

YA
1208324

First published in Great Britain by Barrington Stoke Ltd
10 Belford Terrace, Edinburgh EH4 3DQ
Copyright © 2000 Ann Halam
Illustrations © Edmund Bright
The moral right of the author has been asserted in
accordance with the Copyright, Designs and
Patents Act 1988
ISBN 1-902260-57-0
Printed by Polestar AUP Aberdeen Ltd

The publisher gratefully acknowledges general subsidy
from the Scottish Arts Council towards the Barrington Stoke
teenage fiction series

THE SCOTTISH ARTS COUNCIL

A Note from the Author

I always get the ideas for my stories from real life, but usually I have to make the ghost part up. *The Shadow on the Stairs* is the other way round. I started with a real ghost.

My sister used to live in Kendal, Cumbria in a tall, thin house with narrow, crooked stairs leading up to the attics. The house was supposed to be haunted. When her son was little he once told her that he had seen a strange girl in a long dress crying on the stairs.

I once slept in the room that is Joe's bedroom in the story, but I didn't see the ghost. All the rest of the details are made up.

Contents

1   The House on the Corner   1

2   Diane   7

3   A Shattered Dream   15

4   The Ghost Tape   23

5   Doomed   31

6   The Bricked-up Window   37

7   The Storm   43

8   Maisie Day   53

9   Fear In The Dark   59

10 Maisie's Room   65

Joe

Diane

Dad

Chapter 1
The House on the Corner

"Your house is haunted," said Emma.

"Don't be stupid," said Joe.

Emma was one of Joe's friends at school. They were on the bus going home and they were sitting at the back on the top deck. It was their favourite place, but they didn't usually manage to get it because the Year

1

Tens always grabbed the best seats. This afternoon their school bus was quieter than usual, because a lot of the older kids were off on a school trip.

"No, it's true," said Emma. "My auntie used to live in your street. She's told me about that house, the one on the corner. The one where you live. It's been haunted for years and years. If you step on the ghost's shadow, you are doomed. If it looks at you, you'll die."

"I don't care," said Joe. "I'm not scared of ghosts, anyway."

Joe's Mum and Dad had split up. He lived with his Dad now. They'd recently moved out of their flat and into a house.

When he got off the bus, Joe walked down the street where he lived and stood looking at his house. It was winter, so it was already getting dark. The house was tall and thin, with little old-fashioned windows and chimneys that looked like skinny, oversized flowerpots.

He wondered if Emma's story could be true. Joe's bedroom was on the top floor of the tall, thin house. There was a flight of stairs outside his door that led to the attics. Joe's Dad was planning to do something up there, maybe make a workshop for himself and an extra bedroom, but at the moment those rooms were empty.

That night when he went to bed, Joe

stood outside his room and looked up the attic stairs. There wasn't any carpet on them yet, they were bare wood. He was wondering about Emma's ghost story. If there was a creepy place in the house, this was it.

The old staircase was narrow and there were no windows in the walls on either side. In the light from the window on the landing Joe could see a fuzzy shadow lying on the pale wood of the steps, about halfway up. As he stared it seemed to grow sharper and darker, until it looked exactly like the shadow of a small person. Except that there was nobody there.

Joe felt frightened. It was only a shadow, but somehow it looked evil. Yet he was

strangely tempted to go and tread on that dark outline.

"Don't be daft," he said to himself, out loud. "There's nothing there." His voice sounded weird and echoey in the silence at the top of the old house. But he wasn't going to get scared of a shadow, even if there didn't seem to be anything causing it.

Emma liked making things up. She often told whoppers. He would bet she'd never *had* an aunt who had lived in this street. She'd probably made up the story of Joe's house being haunted, right there on the bus.

He decided he would put the ghost idea out of his mind. He would concentrate on the good things about moving, like having more space for all his things. He was

planning to decorate his own room and make it look really good.

Chapter 2
Diane

Joe got on well with his Dad's girlfriend, Diane. She was pretty and he liked the way she dressed and the way Dad always seemed to be in a good mood when she was around. He also liked the way she didn't try to take over Joe's life.

Dad had had other girlfriends who were pushy and worked too hard at being friends

with Joe, or else they made him feel
unwanted.

Diane wasn't like that. When she came
to visit, life went on as normal. If Joe went
off to his room to listen to music or play
the latest football game on his Playstation,
that was fine. If Joe and Dad wanted to do
things together, the way they often did, she
wasn't offended.

It was a big shock when he found out
what was going on. It was a Saturday, a
few weeks after they'd moved into the new
house. Joe was still thinking about what
Emma had said about the ghost. Every
night, he looked for that shadow on the
attic stairs. Sometimes he thought he could
see it, sometimes he thought he couldn't.
He told himself he wasn't scared but he

wished he could get the idea that it was evil out of his mind.

He didn't suspect that something much worse than seeing a strange shadow was about to happen to him.

****

It started out by being a really good Saturday. In the morning Joe was playing in a match for his under-fifteens football team. Dad and Diane both came and watched and Joe had a good game. He did some excellent tackling and he set up the team's striker for the winning goal. It felt great to be playing well with two people cheering for him on the sideline.

In the afternoon Joe went round to his friend Mark's house. When he came home, Dad and Diane were in the kitchen, obviously preparing a special meal. They had a bottle of wine open.

Joe looked at the wine and the fancy food and Dad and Diane's smiling faces. Suddenly, although he still didn't know why, he had a bad feeling. Those smiles were too big and bright.

The three of them sat down to eat together, with a tablecloth and the best china and the good knives and forks.

That's when they told him. Diane was coming to live with Joe and his Dad. She was going to move in straight away, it was all fixed up.

"Why didn't you tell me before?" demanded Joe.

Diane and his Dad gave each other a worried look.

"We thought it would be better to get everything sorted out first ..." said Dad.

"You didn't tell me because you knew I'd hate to have her move in," shouted Joe.

"Joe!" snapped Dad, looking horrified. "Don't talk like that!"

"We don't need *her!*" shouted Joe. "We can look after ourselves! Why do we have to have a stranger moving in? How could you do this to me, Dad? I hate you!"

Joe shoved back his chair and stood up. He moved too fast and accidentally pulled on the tablecloth. Everything went flying – food and plates and glasses.

Joe stood there, looking at Diane's shocked face and Dad's angry face. A huge stain of red wine spread over the white tablecloth, that was now lying in a crumpled heap on the floor at his feet. He hadn't meant to do it, but the whole mess looked exactly the way he felt, shattered and confused and twisted up inside.

He ran out of the room and straight up to his bedroom and slammed the door.

After a few minutes he heard footsteps. His Dad knocked on the door and said in a

gentle voice, "Joe, come down and talk about it. I'm sorry we gave you a shock."

"Leave me alone," said Joe. "I'll be all right. Please, leave me alone for a bit."

After a few more minutes, the footsteps went away.

Chapter 3
A Shattered Dream

Joe's Mum had married again. She lived nearby and Joe often went to see her. He stayed with her when his Dad had to be away overnight for work.

He knew she loved him, but he felt she was not really 'Joe's Mum' anymore. She had a new life and a new family. It was as if

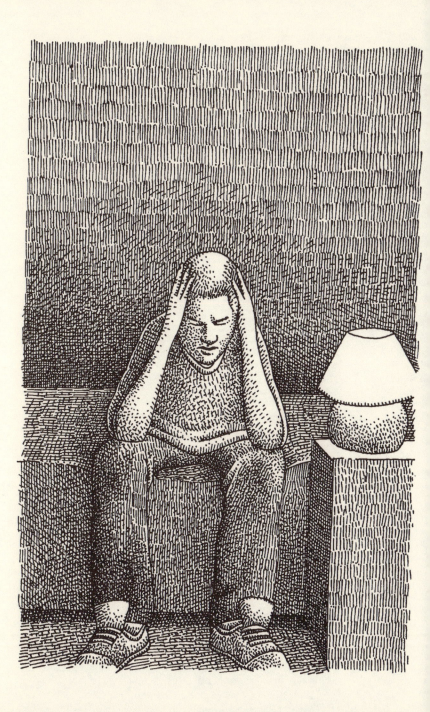

she'd turned into someone else. When he went to stay with her he had to share with his stepbrother. He didn't have a room of his own and that made him feel he didn't belong.

He had felt safe with his Dad. He'd believed that they would live together and look after each other until Joe grew up. He would always have a place where he belonged. Now that dream was shattered.

He sat on his bed thinking how stupid he had been. He should have guessed what was happening from the first moment Dad said they were moving into this house.

The house was far too big for two people. Now Diane would move in. Diane and Joe's Dad would have children. They

would be a new family and Joe wouldn't fit in.

Dad was very kind to Joe after that Saturday. He never said a word about the broken glasses or the mess. But Diane was still going to move in, there was no question about that.

Diane and Dad both explained they'd been sure he'd be pleased. They thought Joe and Diane got on so well. They'd hoped that telling him would be a celebration. They tried to get him to talk about everything and explain why he felt so bad.

But Joe was so angry and miserable, he couldn't talk about his feelings. He told them he was OK and he would get used to the idea. He didn't make any more scenes.

So Diane moved in one day when Joe was at school. She brought all her stuff – her CD collection, her clothes, pictures, books and kitchen things – even some furniture. Wherever he looked, he saw Diane's things. Already, it seemed as if Joe didn't belong in this house any more.

"I'm hoping for the best, Joe," she said. "I like you and I know you like me. I'm certain that this will work and soon we'll get on well again."

Joe let her think what she liked. But really, right from that first day she moved in, he was determined he was going to get her out.

****

At first he tried to think of cunning ways to make her and Dad split up. Maybe he could send Diane flowers and chocolates from 'a secret admirer', so Dad would think she had another boyfriend.

Then he remembered the ghost story. He knew Diane was scared of ghosts. She never watched horror movies and she was terrified of the dark. If she believed the house was haunted, she wouldn't want to live in it.

This seemed like a better idea, less cruel than trying to break them up. Diane could go on being Dad's girlfriend, but she'd be staying in her own place again. Everything would be the way it was before she moved in.

But how was he going to get her to believe the house was haunted? He'd have to be sneaky. Just telling her there was supposed to be a ghost wouldn't be much good.

Luckily, he was soon able to think of a plan and he was sure it would work.

Chapter 4
The Ghost Tape

Joe had been interested in making sound recordings for years. He had a very good music centre that his Dad had bought for him on his twelfth birthday. He'd worked hard finding out how to create all kinds of different sound effects.

Last term the Drama teacher, who knew about his hobby, had asked him to make a tape of background noises for a school play.

The tape had worked really well. The teacher had told him he'd done "an excellent, professional job". Joe was proud of that. His dream was to be a sound engineer one day and work in TV.

If Joe used his skills to make a tape of ghostly noises, it wouldn't be stupid-sounding fake groans and howls and rattling chains. He knew he could produce something truly spooky and frightening.

For days he went around trying out spooky sound effects in his head. He thought about how he would produce them and how he'd fit them together. Then he

made the tape, finding times when he was alone in the house. It took hours of work, but at last he knew he had it exactly right. Now all he needed was an opportunity to test his plan.

His chance soon came. Dad had to be away overnight. In the old days Joe would have gone to stay with his Mum. This time he would stay at home. Joe and Diane would be alone in the house all night.

Diane had not come in from work when he arrived home from school that day.

He sneaked into Diane and Dad's room, loaded the tape into his old radio-alarm cassette player and set it to start playing at 1.30 am. The player had batteries so he didn't need to plug it in.

He hid it in the back of Dad's wardrobe, behind a row of shoes. At 1.30 am Diane would be lying in bed, either asleep or falling asleep.

The first thing she'd hear would be a series of sharp raps, like someone knocking on a door.

Then she'd hear soft footsteps, then there'd be a pause ... then the sound of someone breathing ... then another pause ... then evil muttering and rustling sounds ... more breathing, some sobbing, whimpering noises ...

And so on, for half an hour.

Joe had put an echo on the tape and used other tricks so it would be very hard for

Diane to work out where the noises were coming from. The breathing and sobbing should sound as if they were right by her and the pauses would make it more frightening. She'll be lying there too terrified to move, he thought. Waiting to see if it started up again, waiting for something worse ...

He went to bed feeling very pleased with himself. Tonight was only the beginning. He planned to hide the cassette player in different places around the house. He would load it with different mixes of his spooky effects.

Whenever Dad wasn't around, Diane would hear ghostly noises. She'd soon be a bag of nerves. She'd tell Dad, but Dad didn't

believe in ghosts and he would never hear the noises, so he wouldn't believe her. She'd have to leave and Joe would have won.

But Joe couldn't get to sleep. He kept thinking about Diane, lying there terrified. He also started thinking about his Dad and how furious he would be if he found out what Joe had done.

About midnight, he got out of bed. He'd realised that trying to scare Diane was a crazy, nasty idea that would land him in big trouble. He had to get that cassette player back. He knew Diane was still in the living room. There'd been a film she wanted to watch on television and it didn't finish until after midnight.

He opened his door carefully and looked up the attic stairs. He always looked up the stairs, to see if the strange shadow was there, whenever he came out of his room. He couldn't help himself.

But this time there was no shadow. The light from his bedroom slanted upwards, into the dark. He could see the dim transparent form of a little girl in a long, white nightie. She was standing with her back to him halfway up the stairs. Her brown hair was hanging down in straggly locks.

Joe felt as if the blood had drained out of him. He stepped back into his room and shut the door. He went and sat on the side of his bed. He was cold and shaking all over.

He closed his hands into fists so his fingernails were digging into his palms, but he couldn't stop the shaking.

He was doomed. He was sure Dad and Diane would find out about his stupid trick and he'd be in terrible trouble. But there was nothing he could do. There was no way, no possible way, he could leave his room while that dim figure of the girl was standing out there. He would have to turn his back on the ghost and the thought of it made him feel sick.

In the end he managed to get back into bed. He didn't sleep much.

Chapter 5
Doomed

The next morning when he went down to breakfast, his worst fears had come true. His old radio-alarm cassette player was standing there on the breakfast bar, next to the boxes of cereal.

"I was awake half the night," said Diane, grinning at him. "Scared out of my wits,

with the bedside light on. But in the morning I got sensible and searched the joint."

"Are you going to tell Dad?" asked Joe, miserably.

"Do you think I should?" said Diane.

Joe knew he should beg her not to tell his Dad anything.

But she was the enemy and he couldn't bring himself to plead for his life. So he shrugged and said, "Do what you like. I don't care."

Diane told Joe's Dad and of course he was furious. When Diane saw how angry he was, she tried to defend Joe. She said the

tape was very clever. It was only a joke. She was so glad the ghostly noises hadn't been real that she couldn't be angry with Joe.

But it was too late, the damage was done. Joe's Dad grounded him for a week, but that was nothing. The way his Dad looked at him was much, much worse. For days, it seemed as if they would never be friends again.

Joe had known it was going to be like this. Diane had moved in and Joe's Dad didn't belong to him any more. They were like strangers with each other. He didn't see the ghost on the stairs again. He almost managed to tell himself that he'd been imagining things.

But the wicked shadow was still there, sometimes. And sometimes, when he was alone in his room after dark, he'd get a weird, icy feeling. Then he knew that if he opened his door and looked up the stairs, he would see that ghostly figure again. She would have her back to him, same as before. This time she would look round, over her shoulder. He'd see her dead face peering down at him and then he was sure he would die or go mad.

Of course he never opened the door. But he felt strangely tempted. It was as if something was pulling him towards horrible destruction.

There was no one he could tell. He just had to put up with it.

He remembered that Emma had said, "If
you step on the ghost's shadow, you are
doomed". He wondered if he'd stepped on
the shadow long ago, without knowing it.
Maybe he'd trodden on the wicked shadow
one night before he knew it was there.
When he and Dad had first moved in and
when they had still been happy together.
Maybe that was when everything in his life
had started to go wrong.

Chapter 6
The Bricked-up Window

Gradually Dad stopped being angry. Christmas that year wasn't great for Joe, but it wasn't totally miserable either.

The weeks went by and winter passed. Joe still didn't like having Diane in the house and hated it when she started redecorating. Every change she made

seemed to be pushing Joe further away from his Dad. But he knew he had to accept the situation.

When he had to be with her, he tried to behave normally. He just kept out of her way whenever he could. He spent a lot of time alone in his room. He thought about the old days and wished he could have them back.

Then his Dad had to go away on another overnight trip. He told Joe about it when they were out in the garden one evening. Dad was pruning rosebushes.

Joe was wearing a pair of thick work gloves. He was carrying the prunings to a heap at the bottom of the garden, where Dad was going to make a bonfire.

Dad said, "I know you still don't get on with Diane. You've made that very clear. Do you want to go and stay with your Mum that night?"

Dad didn't often have to take overnight trips. It was the first time this had happened since the awful business of the ghostly noises.

Joe felt his cheeks go red. He turned away so his Dad wouldn't see his face.

****

It was a beautiful, early spring evening. The sky was still blue, though the air was getting chilly. He could hear Diane singing

as she painted the kitchen walls. The
windows were open to let the paint fumes
escape. She had a nice voice.

The garden of the tall, thin old house
was full of bulb shoots – snowdrops,
daffodils and tulips were popping up
everywhere. They had been planted by the
people who used to live here.

Joe suddenly knew how much he wanted
to be happy again, even if it meant having
to live with Diane. "No," he said. "That's all
right. I'll stay with Diane. We'll keep each
other company." It was the nearest he could
come to saying he was sorry.

He looked up. The old house seemed to
be leaning down over the garden, as if it
was listening. Just under the roof, where

the attics were, Joe saw something that he'd never noticed before. It was an outline in the brickwork that looked like a blocked-up window. That's funny, he thought — there aren't any bricked-up windows in the attics. But he hadn't been up there since he and Dad first moved in, so maybe he was remembering this wrong.

The funny thing was, Dad and Diane never went up to the attics either. It was as if something warned them to keep away from the haunted stairs, even though they had never seen the ghost, or the wicked shadow.

"Joe? What's up?"

Joe realised that his Dad had been trying to hand him another bundle of rose

prunings and Joe had been standing there ignoring him.

"Nothing," said Joe. "I was daydreaming."

Chapter 7
The Storm

Next morning, Joe's Dad came down to breakfast with his overnight bag already packed. His trip would last two days. Joe and Diane wouldn't see him until late the next evening.

His Dad said, "You've got my mobile phone number, in case anything goes wrong." Then he gave Diane a kiss and Joe a hug. "Look after my girl for me," he said to Joe. "I'm depending on you."

Joe nodded and smiled as best he could. He felt as if he was on trial.

It was a Tuesday. Joe had football training after school, so it was past five o'clock by the time he came home.

Diane was already back from work. She was out in the garden, looking up at the sky. The day had been strangely warm. Now there were heavy clouds, the colour of bruises, gathering overhead.

"I think we're going to have a

thunderstorm," she said.

"Can you have thunderstorms in February?" asked Joe. He thought thunder belonged in summer.

"I don't know, but it looks as if we're going to get one," said Diane.

They went indoors. "Shall I cook some dinner for both of us," said Diane, "or would you rather get a takeaway?"

Joe remembered when he and his Dad used to do the cooking together. It hurt to think that time was over forever. He didn't mind eating meals Diane had cooked when Dad was here. But if she cooked for him when Dad wasn't here, it would be like

admitting she'd taken over. It would be a big defeat. But he swallowed his pride.

"If you feel like cooking, there's not much point in getting a takeaway," he mumbled.

"Great. How about a fry-up and chips?" offered Diane.

"That's not very healthy," said Joe.

"I know, but I'm sure you had a healthy lunch," said Diane, with a cheeky grin. "Let's give ourselves a night off from being sensible."

While Joe had a shower to wash off the football mud, Diane cooked. They ate together at the kitchen table. By the time

they'd finished eating, rain was rattling on the kitchen windows.

As Joe got up to put the plates in the sink, there was a low, soft rumble in the distance.

"Thunder," said Diane, uneasily. "I was right."

When he'd done the washing up, Joe went off to his own room to do his homework. But he never had much homework on a Tuesday.

After he'd finished it, he sat staring at the wall above his desk. The thunder was getting closer and the rain and wind sounded wild. It was a powerful storm.

He thought about Diane, downstairs, alone. He knew she was frightened of thunderstorms. He sighed. It was no use, he'd have to go and keep her company. They could watch television, so he wouldn't have to talk to her.

"Hello," he said, as he walked into the living room. "I finished my homework. What's on?"

"Hi," said Diane. "N-nothing much. There's a film on later that might be good."

Joe sat down. They watched the news together, but did not say much to each other. That was the good thing about Diane, she never chattered for the sake of talking.

Joe began to relax. He found himself remembering how he'd used to like her, before she moved in.

Suddenly, they heard several loud raps. The sounds didn't come from the front door. They were very close.

Joe nearly jumped out of his skin. He stared at Diane and she stared back at him.

They heard soft footsteps pattering, as if they were right there in the living room.

"I'm not doing it!" yelled Joe, "It's not me! I'm not playing tricks!" Joe thought somehow the spooky tape must have turned itself on. But he didn't know where it was. He hadn't seen his old radio-alarm cassette

player since he'd played that trick on Diane. His Dad had kept it.

He jumped up, looking around wildly.

The rapping started again, mixed with sounds like a child sobbing. The hairs on the back of Joe's neck were standing on end and he had that horrible, icy feeling.

"I'm not doing it!" he repeated, desperately. "It's not me!"

"I know," gasped Diane, her eyes huge with fear. "Joe, don't worry, I ..."

Whatever else she said was lost in a great crash of thunder.

The television picture vanished and all the lights went out.

Chapter 8
Maisie Day

Diane grabbed Joe's hand. Together they stumbled to the kitchen. It was completely dark in there. The wind howled and the rain at the windows sounded like machine gun fire. Another huge clap of thunder was followed by a vivid bolt of lightning.

For a flash of a second, Joe saw Diane scrabbling in a kitchen drawer. Then the kitchen was black again, but she'd found some candles and some matches. She lit two candles and put them on the kitchen counter.

Now they could see each other – two frightened faces surrounded by darkness.

The raps came again, and the sobbing. The noises seemed to be here in the kitchen.

"Joe," said Diane, breathlessly. "I believe you. I know you're not playing tricks. Your Dad destroyed that tape and I'm sure you wouldn't do that again, anyway."

"Then what's going on?" gasped Joe.

"This is supposed to be a haunted house," said Diane, "I always knew that."

"You knew?" whispered Joe.

"Yes," said Diane.

They each took a candle and sat down on the floor. Their backs were against the doors of the kitchen cupboards. They did not dare to move from the spot.

"It started a hundred years ago," began Diane. "There was a terrible epidemic of scarlet fever in the town. A little girl, called Maisie Day, was living in this house. She was eight years old. She caught the fever. Scarlet fever was a very dangerous disease, then. Her Mum and Dad put her in a room by herself, so she wouldn't infect the other

children ..."

Joe gulped. He thought, I've seen her! But he couldn't bring himself to say that out loud, he was too scared. "Why didn't they send her to hospital?" he asked.

"They were too poor. They had a lot of children. People had big families in those days. Maisie had four little brothers and sisters. Her father took the two older ones to stay with their grandmother in the country. Her mother stayed, with the baby and the toddler, and Maisie.

"But Maisie's mother caught the fever herself. No one really knows what happened after that. The neighbours took Maisie's mother to a charity hospital and looked after the little ones.

"Apparently everyone thought Maisie had gone with her father, and her mother was too ill to tell them the truth. So Maisie Day was left behind. And the door to her room was locked. Her mother had kept it locked, so the toddler wouldn't run in there and catch the fever."

"S-so ..." whispered Joe, his voice shaking. "W-what happened to her?"

"She died, Joe. Her mother and father found her dead in that room when they came back. No one knows which room it was. But ever since then, the people who've lived in this house — not all of them, just some of them — have heard her crying in the night and hammering on a locked door."

Diane got hold of Joe's hand. "That's why I was so scared by your tape," she explained. "Because I knew the story of poor Maisie Day. But I would never have told your Dad about that trick you played on me, if I had known how angry he'd be. I just didn't think. I've wanted to tell you I was sorry about that."

"I thought it would make you move out, because you were afraid of ghosts," said Joe.

"I *am* afraid," said Diane. "Maybe your Dad is, too. Maybe that's why he was so angry. But Joe, think about it. She's only a little girl." Diane stood up. "If a lost child cries like that, it's because she wants to be found. Come on, let's go and find her."

Chapter 9
Fear In The Dark

All the time Joe and Diane had been talking, there had been no noise but the raging of the storm. As Diane stood up, a whimpering sound seemed to come from outside in the hall.

"Let's take torches," said Joe. He didn't like the look of his candle's flickering flame. He felt sure it would go out.

He found two torches in another drawer. They took the candles and matches with them as well and set off. They followed the ghostly noises. It was like a very scary game of hide-and-seek. When they were on the landing outside Diane and Dad's room, they heard pattering footsteps come up behind them.

When they turned around there was nothing. As they looked into Joe's room, the rapping started again downstairs. When they hurried towards that sound, something started muttering and sobbing by the kitchen door ...

There were other sounds too. The worst was a kind of scrabbling and gnawing that gave Joe horrible ideas — about rats and a sick, little girl who couldn't get away.

They crept from room to room, trying every light switch to see if the power had come back on, but it hadn't.

Joe didn't know why he was doing this. He thought Diane's plan was crazy. But anything was better than cowering helplessly in the dark, waiting for something horrible to happen.

As they came upstairs for the third time, Joe distinctly heard soft, rapid breathing right by his ear. He was sure that something passed him, heading for the attics. He didn't think Diane had heard

anything, but this time she wanted to go up there.

"No!" said Joe. He was too scared.

Diane didn't argue. Maybe she felt the same as Joe, as she stood at the bottom of those narrow, dark stairs. Only a fool would dare to go ghost-chasing up there.

They went back to the living room. There was still no power and the storm thundered on. For what seemed a long time, nothing happened. Joe remembered how he'd put pauses between the spooky effects on that stupid tape, to make it more scary. He'd been right about that, he decided.

Then a hand touched his arm. It was a small hand, so cold he could feel it like a

grip of ice through the sleeve of his sweater. He turned his head, terrified of what he might see but unable not to look ...

Diane was sitting beside him, holding her torch in both hands. She was staring at the circle of light it made on the rug.

Beyond Diane, in the open doorway of the room, a strange light that came from nowhere showed him the figure of a girl in a white nightdress. She had her back to him.

Chapter 10
Maisie's Room

Joe had no choice. He couldn't resist. The ghost had come to fetch him and he had to follow. Out into the hall, up the stairs ... and on, up to the attics.

The wild sounds of the storm continued and the light of his torch had turned yellow and feeble. The batteries were running out.

He desperately wanted to turn back, but he couldn't. He pressed himself against the wall, as he climbed those narrow stairs. He was afraid to step on the place where the wicked shadow lay.

Now nothing could save him. He'd reached the door to the attics.

He had to turn the doorknob, open the door and look in. He tried to switch on the light, but nothing happened. His feeble torch beam showed an empty, dusty space.

The ghost stood facing the wall, with her brown hair hanging down. In a moment she would turn and look at him over her shoulder. He would see her dead face.

Joe started to scream. He screamed and screamed. Footsteps came pounding up the narrow stairs ...

"Joe!" cried Diane, "What's happening? Why did you leave me like that?"

He couldn't speak. He grabbed at her, forgetting all his pride.

Diane hugged him hard. "It's OK," she told him, sounding terrified but very brave. "Don't worry, it's OK ..."

At that moment, wonderfully, the light came on. Diane sighed with relief and looked around. There were two attic rooms. This was the bigger one. It was completely empty. "What happened, Joe? Did you see something?"

"Look!" croaked Joe, pointing with a shaking hand.

Diane shook her head. "I can't see anything." She went to the place where he was pointing and looked at the wall. "Joe!" she exclaimed, "I think there was a door here!"

Diane could see nothing, but Joe could still see the dim figure of a little girl. "Don't!" he whispered, horrified. "Don't touch her!"

He watched, paralysed, as the girl's tousled, brown head started to turn. He imagined the hollow cheeks and empty stare of the little girl who had been left alone to die. But he did not see her face.

Diane was in the way. Or maybe at the last moment, he managed to close his eyes.

When he looked again, Diane had passed through the ghost, and the girl was gone. Diane was tearing ruthlessly at the faded wallpaper. The plaster underneath fell off in chunks and revealed the corner of a lock, on the door of a room – perhaps a room that had been hidden for a hundred years?

"I think we've found the place where Maisie Day died," said Diane. She looked solemn but then she smiled at Joe. "We'll come back in daylight and open it up. It's all right, don't be scared. I'm sure this is what she wanted us to find. I'm sure the haunting is over." She laughed. "I'd better

call your Dad. He'll be worried. He knows I hate thunderstorms."

In fact it was the next Saturday before they forced the door open. The small room inside was very bare. There was a window that had been bricked up. And there was a bed – a little, iron-framed bed. In the ancient, dusty, rotten mattress you could still see the hollow imprint of a child's body.

There was nothing else in the room.

Diane said she was going to get the window opened up again. She planned to clean the hidden room out and decorate it. They would use it for something happy and good. She was sure that was the best way to heal the memory of that long ago tragedy.

Maybe Joe and his Dad could have a computer room and a workshop up there together.

Joe's Dad didn't believe in ghosts, but he agreed with her.

There couldn't be any harm in using that room.

Joe hoped they were right.

Barrington Stoke would like to thank all its readers for commenting on the manuscript before publication and in particular:

Hannah Brown
Phillip Caspari
Joanne Johns
Eliza Johns
Brian Matheson
Stewart Nairn
Leigh Peters

Become a Consultant!

Would you like to give us feedback on our titles before they are published? Contact us at the address or website below – we'd love to hear from you!

Barrington Stoke, 10 Belford Terrace, Edinburgh EH4 3DQ
Tel: 0131 315 4933 Fax: 0131 315 4934
E-mail: barringtonstoke@cs.com
Website: www.barringtonstoke.co.uk

More Titles

Playing Against the Odds
by Bernard Ashley

Chris's world is turned upside down by the arrival of Fiona in his class. His loyalties are torn in two as more and more thefts take place at school. But nothing can prepare Chris for the betrayal that lies ahead ...

To Be A Millionaire
by Yvonne Coppard

The news that a famous film director is in town sets Jack's mind racing. At last, he thinks, he's finally got his break! All he has to do is to be in the right place at the right time. This time it's up to him.

Runaway Teacher
by Pete Johnson

Scott thinks teachers are boring. Then a new teacher arrives - a teacher with very different ideas about lessons, rules and school. But when too many rules are broken, Scott learns just how complicated friendship and loyalty can be.

Falling Awake
by Viv French

Danny is cool. The younger kids think they're cool too, but they are just kiddie babes to Danny. He can make easy money out of them. He isn't going to say no to easy money, is he? Not until the day he wakes up on the pavement. Out of it. Trapped. This time Danny's gone too far.

Alien Deeps
by Douglas Hill

When Tal plunges through the protecting field on the edge of the Clear Zone, he knows that he is leaving the only safe place on the planet. Beyond it lies the unknown, a world outside human control. But is the unknown the greatest danger in the alien deeps?